TEAM HERO

ATTACK OF THE BAT ARMY

ADAM BLADE

ORCHARD

MEET TEAM HERO ...

JACK

POWER: Super-strength

LIKES: Ventura City FC

DISLIKES: Bullies

RUBY

POWER: Fire vision

LIKES: Comic books

DISLIKES: Small spaces

DANNY

POWER: Super-hearing

LIKES: Pizza

DISLIKES: Thunder

GENERAL GORE

POWER: Brilliant warrior

LIKES: Carnage

DISLIKES: Unfaithful minions

CONTENTS

PROLOGUE

SHADOWS SURROUNDED the boy as
he stumbled down the corridor. It was
past midnight and Hero Academy was
silent. Shadows filled the doorways
to the empty classrooms, too, and
shrouded the rough stone walls of
the school. But the darkest shadow
of all lurked within the boy's mind. It
was telling him to follow the creature

flying ahead of him.

The terrawing, he thought. He'd
never seen one before, but somehow
he knew what it
was. The
creature
was the size
of a small
eagle, with
bat-like wings
that rustled as it flapped
ahead. Its feet hung down, ending
in sharp claws. Its beak was long
and curved. On its back was a metal
barrel.

Some kind of weapon, the boy

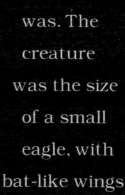

thought, his spine tingling with fear.

The terrawing glided down a flight of steps, and the boy shuffled after it, trying to keep up. It swooped through a set of doors, out into the cobbled courtyard. When the boy saw the great blackened circle in the centre, he stopped, struck with terror.

The portal.

Inside, frozen stone monsters wielded swords and axes. Skeleton creatures raised spears above their heads. They were horrifying, but the boy had seen them many times before. What really frightened him was the swirl of black shadow rising from the edge of the portal.

The terrawing hovered beside him. It screeched angrily, jabbing its beak towards the portal. The boy knew it was telling him to go closer.

Helplessly, he stumbled forward.

The shadow rising from the portal shimmered until it had turned into a tall figure. He wore a helmet and a long cloak that flowed like smoke over his broad shoulders. Beyond the figure, the boy could make out a gloomy landscape, dotted with nightmarish figures tending fire pits and forging weapons. A fortress of twisted towers loomed in the distance.

The boy knew that this was the underground realm of Noxx and that the tall man was its leader, General Gore.

"How weak you humans are," said

the General. His red eyes were locked on the boy's. "So easy to control."

Horrified, the boy started to back away. *I won't listen to him*, he thought. *I've got to fight the shadow inside me ...*

General Gore's eyes flashed and he lifted a hand. A blast of darkness flowed from his palm and surrounded the boy, who felt the shadow in his mind growing larger. Suddenly he knew that he would do whatever General Gore asked.

"That's better," said the General in menacing tones. "You will make a fine servant of Noxx yet."

The boy nodded helplessly. "What is your bidding, Master?"

"The Shadow Sword," the General said. "Where is it?"

The sword had been lost by General Gore hundreds of years ago, when he had last tried to invade the surface of the earth. Only Gore could use the sword — until now ...

"The Chosen One has got it," said the boy.

General Gore flinched. "And just who is this Chosen One?" he hissed.

The prophecy surfaced within the boy's memory: *Darkness will rise and conquer light, unless the Chosen One joins the fight.* For a moment, the words made him want to fight the shadow, to defeat General Gore and his Noxxian army for ever …

The moment passed.

"His name's Jack Beacon," the boy said. "He's a student at Hero Academy."

General Gore narrowed his red eyes. "Jack Beacon," he repeated. He clenched his gloved fists. "Soon this Chosen One will be destroyed! And Hero Academy too!"

The image of General Gore and Noxx swirled and vanished. With a beat of its wings, the terrawing flew

away into the night. The boy was
alone in the courtyard, shivering in
the darkness.

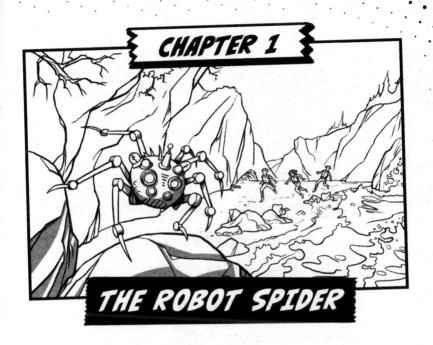

CHAPTER 1

THE ROBOT SPIDER

JACK BEACON raced across the beach towards the towering cliff-face. Gulls screeched overhead and the surf crashed against the rocky shoreline. Beside him ran his friends, Danny and Ruby. Jack saw the robotic spider they were chasing skitter over the shingle. It dived for

cover in a pile of boulders at the foot
of the cliff.

Ruby leapt up on to a boulder,
shaking her curly black hair from her
eyes as she searched for the metal
creature. "Where did it go?"

"Careful," Danny puffed. "Those
rocks look slippery."

Ruby ignored him. "There!" she
cried.

Jack watched, impressed, as
Ruby sprang lightly from boulder
to boulder. She wasn't scared of
anything.

"Looks like we'd better follow her,"
said Jack.

Danny groaned. "Can't we have a rest first?"

"We've got to be back at school by lunchtime, remember?" said Jack. "So we've only got twenty minutes left to catch the spider."

Danny rubbed his eyes and Jack noticed how tired his friend looked.

"Are you OK?" Jack asked.

"I didn't sleep well," said Danny. "You probably kept the whole dormitory awake with your snoring."

Jack gave him a friendly shove. "It's not my fault you've got super-hearing! Anyway, I don't snore."

"How do you know?" Danny said,

but he was grinning. "I'm definitely wearing earplugs tonight."

They clambered over the pile of rocks until they caught up with Ruby. She was crouched next to a huge boulder.

"The spider's crawled under there," she said. "I can't get it out."

Danny nudged Jack. "I bet you can!"

Jack took a firm grip of the boulder with his scaly, golden hands. His super-strength tingled through him like an electric current as he lifted the enormous rock over his head.

Before Jack had started at Hero Academy, just two weeks ago, he'd

always worn
gloves to stop
people seeing his
hands. But now
he was proud of
them. Everyone at
Hero Academy was
different, all with
some kind of special power.

Carefully, he placed the boulder to
one side.

"Thanks, Jack!" Ruby said. "Look!"

The spider was half buried in sand,
crouched low on its spiky metal legs.
Ruby reached to grab it – but it
scuttled away with lightning speed,

heading for the cliff-face.

"Come on!" Jack shouted.

They dashed after it. The spider stopped at the base of the cliff. It twitched its tiny antennae.

Jack drew the Shadow Sword from his belt. It felt light and comfortable in his hand, like it was meant to be there. Jack had pulled the blade from solid rock, in the basement beneath the school, then used the weapon to defeat Zarnik, one of General Gore's warriors. Chancellor Rex, headmaster of Hero Academy, had told Jack that the sword once belonged to the General himself.

Jack pointed the blade at the spider and crept towards it. "Almost ..." he muttered. But when he was just one step away, the robot scuttled straight up the cliff, out of sight.

Danny ran his hands through his floppy dark hair. "You've got to be joking!"

Ruby was already climbing up the sheer cliff-face. "What are you two waiting for?" she yelled down. "Do you want Olly's team to catch their spider first?"

This time Jack and Danny both groaned. If Olly and his team won, they'd never hear the end of it.

"We're coming!" they yelled together.

Despite Jack's super-strength, the climb wasn't easy. The cliff was slippery and his feet kept sliding off the footholds. Seagulls shrieked and swooped around them. As they climbed higher, Jack could see the island's rugged coast curving towards a black fortress, half hidden by clouds — Hero Academy.

"Can you see the spider yet?" he called up to Ruby. She shook her head.

Beside Jack, Danny went still. He pushed back his hair, revealing large ears that were pointed like a bat's.

"I can hear it," Danny said. "There!"

He pointed up at a ledge of rock
jutting from the cliff. The spider was
clinging to it.

Around the spider's ledge, the cliff-
face was as smooth as glass. There
were no handholds.

"How are we going to get it?" Ruby

wondered aloud.

"Trust your powers," said a voice next to them.

Jack looked around, startled, to see a fourth figure clinging to the cliff — a dark-skinned woman with bright purple hair. It was Ms Steel, one of their teachers. She could teleport and had a habit of turning up when she was least expected.

"Er, hello, Ms Steel," said Jack.

"Trust your powers," Ms Steel said again, with a mysterious smile. "Remember."

Then she vanished.

Jack blinked. "What did she mean?"

Danny frowned thoughtfully, looking up at the spider again. "I think I know," he said slowly. "Ruby, can you blast the ledge?"

Ruby grinned. "No problem."

Her orange eyes began to glow. With a sizzle, streams of burning flames shot from them, slicing right through the ledge of rock. It plummeted down, taking the spider with it.

Jack shot out his hand as it fell past. His golden fingers closed around the spider, plucking it from the rock, which smashed on to the beach below. "Got it!"

Danny whooped. "Good catch!"

The robot powered down, curling itself into a tight ball. Jack stowed it safely in his backpack, and they began climbing down the way they'd come.

"I just hope we've beaten Olly," said Ruby. "He'll be so—"

"Shhh," interrupted Danny suddenly. "Something's coming. I can hear it."

He was looking out to sea. Jack followed his gaze. On the horizon glittered the skyscrapers of Ventura City — Jack's home. Then Jack spotted something hurtling towards them. It was the size of an eagle, but as it flew closer, Jack realised it wasn't an ordinary bird at all. Its bat-like wings beat furiously and its long, cruel beak was open wide. Strapped to the creature's back was a strange metal tube.

"What is it?" he breathed.

A bolt of blue light shot from the metal tube, sizzling towards them.

Boom!

The ball of light struck the cliff-face with a blast so loud, it seemed to have exploded inside Jack's head. A shower of bright sparks almost blinded him.

"We're under attack!" Jack yelled, ears ringing. "Let's go!"

WINGED TERROR

JACK AND his friends scrambled down the cliff. The creature soared past them, so close Jack could see the evil gleam in its eyes. It circled around.

It's getting ready to fire again, Jack realised.

"Cover your ears!" he yelled to Ruby and Danny.

A second bolt of light slammed into the cliff, sending rocks scattering down.

BOOM!

Jack's ears were screaming. Before he had time to recover, the creature fired a third blast.

BOOM!

Jack winced as it exploded to his right, sending a blizzard of rock fragments into his face. But it was the noise of the explosion that really hurt. It seemed to tear at his ears like a thousand shrieking seagulls. Danny let out a moan of pain.

Poor Danny! Jack thought. His

super-hearing must make this so
much worse.

They reached the bottom of the cliff and ran across the beach.

"I can hear more of them coming," Danny said, gasping.

Jack led his friends behind a clump of boulders, just as a flock of the creatures passed overhead. They fired a flurry of bolts, which smashed into the rocks all around them. Danny crouched down, his head in his hands.

"I really wish I had those earplugs now," he groaned.

"We definitely need something," muttered Jack. He switched on Hawk, the Oracle device attached to his ear. It was an Oral Response and Combat Learning Escort, and every student at Hero Academy had one.

"Hello, Jack," said Hawk. *"I see we're at the beach. Lovely weather for it. What can I help you with?"*

"What are those flying things?" Jack asked.

A visor slid over Jack's eyes and zoomed in on a swooping creature. A grid appeared over the image and technical data began scrolling at the side of the screen.

"Those are terrawings," Hawk replied cheerfully. *"Origin: Noxx. Wingspan:*

SKWARK!

two metres. Weapons: blasters that fire bolts of pure sonic energy. The sound can reach over two hundred decibels. That's very loud," he added helpfully.

"You don't say," Jack replied.

The flock shrieked overhead, unleashing another barrage of sonic bolts. The noise was so terrible, Jack had to jam his fingers into his ears.

"Anything you can do to stop it?" he asked.

"Why, certainly. Engaging sonic defenders."

Jack felt a plasma strap extend from the earpiece and reach into his other ear. Instantly the worst of the sound was cut out and Jack felt a wave of relief. He told the others to do the same and Danny's face immediately brightened.

"Thanks," he said, wiping sweat from his forehead.

"What now?" Ruby asked. "Should

we try to fight them?"

Jack shook his head. "They're terrawings from Noxx," he explained, "which means General Gore must be up to something. I think I've got a plan — but we'll have to break cover."

Danny's eyes widened. "Maybe it's just my sonic defenders," he said, "but it sounded like you said we're going back out there."

Jack nodded. "How else are we going to catch one of the terrawings?"

"You want to *catch* one?" Danny asked, eyes bulging.

"Of course," Jack said. "We need to take it to Chancellor Rex. He'll know what to do."

The flock of terrawings swooped past them, then back out to sea. The creatures turned, getting ready to strike again.

"What are we waiting for?" said Ruby, leaping up.

Jack and Danny followed her from their hiding place. Fear clutched at Jack's chest as the flock shrieked angrily and flew towards them. He heard a sizzle and crack as Ruby shot two beams of flame at the oncoming flock. The terrawings scattered in a panic of flapping wings. One of them flew low to the beach — and Jack

grabbed it.

The creature's skin was cold
and clammy. Jack fought back his
disgust. He unclipped the sonic
blaster from its back and stuffed
the struggling terrawing into his
backpack, along with the robot spider.

It thrashed there for a moment, then was still.

Meanwhile, the rest of the flock had regrouped. Ruby shot more fiery beams, keeping them at bay as the three friends sprinted along the zigzagging path that snaked up the hillside to Hero Academy.

Jack's heart lifted as he saw the strong stone walls. They'd be safe inside. He risked a quick glance behind and was relieved to see that the terrawing flock had given up the chase.

"They're flying back out to sea," Ruby said, panting. "Where do you think they're going?"

"Far away from here, I hope," said Danny. "I wonder if the other teams are back yet?"

Inside Jack's backpack, the Noxxian creature shrieked. "We're probably last," Jack said. "But I bet Olly hasn't caught a terrawing!"

CHAPTER 3

A DANGEROUS PLAN

JACK STILL felt like pinching
himself whenever he thought about
his new life at Hero Academy. The
black stone walls rose into the low
clouds. On each of the four towers
a flag flapped in the stiff sea breeze.
The Hero Academy flag was a white
lion on a green background, and in

class he'd learned that the lion stood for courage. The green represented the earth, which Hero Academy had defended for a thousand years.

They went through the gate and into the courtyard. Frozen into the wall of the school was Raptrix, a dead Noxx warrior. He was a gigantic, armoured lizard with clawed forearms and a spiked weapon. The sight of him always made Jack shudder.

There were groups of boys and girls dotted around, some Jack's age, others older. A few were in Red House, like Jack. Other students were in Blue House with Danny, and some in Yellow House, as Ruby was. The rest of the students were in Green House. They all wore silver bodysuits with patches that matched their house colour.

A boy in a Green House uniform with jet-black hair was laughing with a group of friends. He smirked when he caught Jack's eye.

"Great," muttered Jack. "Here comes Olly."

The boy swaggered over. "Thought you'd got lost, Beacon. We brought back our spider ages ago. What took you so long?"

"None of your business," Ruby

snapped at him.

Jack's backpack rustled. Olly stared at it suspiciously. "What've you got in there?"

"Maybe you should show him," said Danny. "It must be hungry by now."

Jack fought back a laugh. He strode past Olly and into the school building, Danny and Ruby close behind. They passed classrooms full of high-tech weapons and equipment and took a lift to the very top of the North Tower. They stepped out in front of the door to Chancellor Rex's study.

Jack was about to knock when the door swung open by itself.

"Come in," came a voice from inside. Chancellor Rex was sitting at a large desk with a computer and piles of books on it. His wrinkled face creased into a smile. "What can I do for you?" he asked.

"We were hunting for spiders—" Jack said.

"There were all these bat-creatures—" said Ruby at the same time.

"They were so *loud*—" Danny was saying.

Chancellor Rex held up a palm for silence. "Jack, why don't you open that backpack and show me what you've found?" he suggested.

Jack glanced at his friends. *How did the Chancellor know ...?* He put the backpack on the desk. The terrawing started thrashing again. Jack pulled the zip open and it burst out of the bag and lurched around the room, screeching loudly. It swooped low over Danny, sending him diving to the floor, and snapped at a plate of biscuits, swallowing them, along with half the plate.

Chancellor Rex held up his other hand, which was sheathed in a shimmering plasma gauntlet, like a liquid metal glove. It crackled with energy. The terrawing was sucked through the air towards it, like it was being hoovered up. In just a moment, it was perched calmly on Chancellor Rex's arm.

Jack gasped in astonishment. Chancellor Rex was full of surprises.

The Chancellor returned the terrawing to the backpack and removed his gauntlet, then went to the window and stared out over the school. "This is very troubling," he said. "If there are terrawings at the school then General Gore must have opcned a second portal."

The three friends looked at each

other in alarm.

"So are these terrawings his new army?" Jack asked.

The Chancellor shook his head. "I believe they're an advance force," he said, "sent by Gore to spy and cause damage before the real army arrives."

He lifted his hands. Jack watched in wonder as light shone from the palms, projecting an image on to the wall. He'd seen the Chancellor do this before, and knew what was coming — a glimpse of the future.

The image showed thousands of screeching terrawings raining sonic missiles down on Hero Academy.

Students ran desperately in all directions, driven mad by the noise.

Danny gasped, and Ruby looked shaken. Jack clenched his fists.

"We can't let Gore do that to us," he said fiercely.

The image disappeared. Chancellor

Rex pressed a button on his desk. An alarm sounded, shrill and urgent.

"The call to arms," Chancellor Rex said. "We must prepare for battle. Go! You must join the others and be ready to fight."

Jack picked up his backpack and they left the Chancellor's study. The image of the school overrun by terrawings was stuck in Jack's mind. Back in the lift at the top of the tower, Ruby hit the ground floor button.

"Jack managed to close the other portal," she said. Her orange eyes were bright. "We just need to find this one and close it too."

"Yeah," said Danny, "but the first portal was right in the middle of the school courtyard. We've got no idea where this one is."

"Maybe not," said Jack, as they stepped out of the lift. "But we know someone who does." He grinned at the other two.

Back in the courtyard, he hurried past Olly and the other students, who were gathering weapons and organising the school defences.

"Running away at the first sign of trouble?" Olly called.

"Go away, Olly!" Jack snapped. He

made his way back to the gate, Danny and Ruby following. They watched, wide-eyed, as he unzipped the backpack again.

"Er, is that a good idea?" said Danny doubtfully.

"Remember how the terrawings kept flying out to sea?" asked Jack. "Well, I think they were going to and from the portal. So if we set our terrawing free …"

"It will lead us there!" Ruby finished with a grin.

The terrawing flapped out of the backpack. It gave a furious screech and flew off.

They charged after it, back down the zigzagging path to the shore. When they reached the bottom, the terrawing had already cleared the island and was flapping away over the sea.

"Quick, before we lose it!" cried Jack.

A row of two-person speedboats was moored at the end of the jetty. Ruby leaped into one. Jack hesitated but then steeled himself.

If closing the portal is the only way to prevent the attack on Hero Academy, then that's what we have to do!

"Come on, Danny!" Jack called.

He looked around and saw his friend bent double, panting for breath and very pale. *Those sonic blasts must have made him feel sick*, he thought. He caught Danny's arm.

"Are you sure you're up to this?" Jack asked. "You can always go back to school—"

Danny shook his head. "No way." He got into a second boat. "Are you steering this thing or shall I?"

Glad to have both of his friends with him, Jack leaped in and fired up the engine. Ruby's boat shot out across the water. Jack pulled back the throttle and his boat roared

alongside hers. Ahead he could see
the black line of the mainland.

"Hawk?" he said.

"What can I help you with, Jack?" his
Oracle asked. *"I see we're now on a*

boat. *I know how to tie over a hundred different knots."*

Jack peered up into the bright sky. "I don't need to tie knots, Hawk. I need to track a terrawing."

"Tracking," Hawk replied. The visor appeared over Jack's eyes. A moment later, a red dot flashed in one corner. *"Terrawing located,"* said Hawk. *"It's a lovely day to be at the seaside. I can locate ice cream shops too."*

"Another time," said Jack. He adjusted the boat's course in the direction of the red dot and roared towards the terrawing's path, Ruby following in her boat.

Her voice sounded in his ear, speaking through her own Oracle. "I know where we're headed," she told him grimly.

Jack twisted round. Ruby was pointing towards a cluster of buildings on a nearby headland. Over them hung a column of black smoke. As they drew closer, Jack saw that among the buildings were great metal vats, twisting pipes, cables and tubes. In the centre was a tall yellow tower.

"Desolate Point," said Ruby's voice. "It's a power station that shut down a couple of years ago. My mum used to work there."

Danny clutched Jack's shoulder. "Look," he said in a tight voice. "There they are!"

Jack looked. What he'd first thought was a black cloud was in fact thousands of twisting, diving shapes, spilling out of the ground and stretching hundreds of feet into the air.

Terrawings!

"Ruby," he said, "we've found the portal."

CHAPTER 4

INSIDE DESOLATE POINT

"MAYBE WE should go back," Danny said doubtfully. "There are too many terrawings for us to fight on our own."

"Hawk, can you alert Chancellor Rex that we've found the portal and need reinforcements?" Jack asked.

"I'd like to, Jack, but an unknown

energy source is interfering with my communication system."

"Looks like it's down to us," Jack told his friends. "We don't have time to go back for help. Look, more terrawings are coming out all the time." He put his hand to the Shadow Sword. Only the sword could close the portals of Noxx — and only Jack could wield the sword. It was up to him to stop this.

They steered their boats to a broken wooden jetty beside Desolate Point and used ropes to tie them to mooring posts. Then they walked into the power station. The ground was overgrown with plants, and broken chunks of masonry lay scattered all around. Many of the crumbling buildings had lost their roofs. The rusty pipes were bent. A long warehouse shielded them from the view of the terrawings and Jack led them along the length of it, avoiding patches of broken glass. They peered around the end of the warehouse at the huge yellow tower.

"It's a reactor," said Ruby. "Mum told me they're full of chemicals — ones that can blow up."

Above it, the spiralling mass of terrawings stretched into the clouds

like a living, twisting skyscraper.
Jack's stomach lurched at the sight of
them.

Then, as one, the creatures turned
towards them. A deafening shriek
filled the air.

Ruby groaned. "They've spotted us!"

"Activate your sonic defenders!"
Jack shouted.

Hawk switched on Jack's own
defenders as hundreds of the
creatures swooped down to attack.
Sonic bolts began pounding the earth
around them, kicking up chunks of
rusty metal and pieces of brick.

BOOM! BOOM! BOOM!

Even with the sonic defenders, the noise was horrible.

"We've got to take cover!" said Ruby.

They ran towards a ruined building and hurried inside. But the sonic blasts slammed into the metal roof, the sounds echoing around them.

Danny was crouched on the ground, his face a mask of horror and pain.

"I can't take any more," he moaned. "The shadow … It's too much …"

Ruby gave him a shake, her orange eyes wide with concern. "Danny, you can't stay here. Your ears can't handle it."

"My ears?" Danny had turned a

shade of grey.

"Ruby's right. This noise is hurting you," said Jack. He pulled Danny to his feet. "Take one of the boats. Go back to school."

"OK," Danny said, staggering outside. "I'll tell the others. Just make sure you win, won't you?"

"Of course we will," said Jack, as they watched Danny stumble his way back to the boats.

Will he even make it back?

"We can't beat them hiding in here," said Ruby. "Let's go!"

She leaped through a broken window. Jack followed, landing

among a swirl of terrawings. He drew the Shadow Sword, swiping at a terrawing that had come too close. Another creature clawed at his shoulder, sending a jolt of pain down his arm. Jack spun round with his blade, slicing at the creatures. Each time he hit one, it exploded into shadow. Ruby shot beams of flame at the creatures, turning them to ash. But more terrawings arrived to replace the ones they destroyed. The sky was as black as night with them.

"We'll never get rid of them all," Jack yelled to Ruby. "We need to close the portal so no more can come out."

"You're right," she shouted back.
"Come on!"

Ducking and weaving their way
through the terrawings, they ran
towards the huge yellow tower where
the creatures had been circling.
The terrawings shrieked with fury,

surrounding Jack and Ruby in a fog
of leathery wings and slashing beaks.

There's got to be a faster way,
thought Jack.

He peered through the flashing
wings and spied a row of tumbledown
warehouses between them and the

yellow tower.

"This way!" he called to Ruby.

Waving his sword to keep the creatures at bay, Jack shoved his way forward, Ruby at his side. At last, they fell through the door of the first warehouse. Jack slammed the door shut before the terrawings could follow.

"Thank goodness for that," said Ruby. "I can hear myself think again."

They ran down the length of the dark building and out of the doors the other side. They ducked through into the next warehouse before the terrawings could follow them. They did the same at the next warehouse, and the next, keeping under cover. Finally they reached the yellow reactor tower. It was covered in signs that said "DANGER! CONTAINS CHEMICALS."

But what held Jack's attention was a huge pool close to the reactor. It swirled with shadow. More terrawings flew out of it, screeching as they joined the others.

"The portal!" cried Ruby. "Quick, Jack — go and close it."

He hurried towards it, holding the Shadow Sword ready. But before he reached the portal, something else rose from it — something much larger than

the terrawings. It was a huge figure. Her body and face were human, but fangs jutted from her mouth and her fingers ended in long talons. She wore black armour and swung a chain with a spiked black ball on the end. Long green hair whipped around her face. A huge pair of wings opened behind her, lifting her high into the air. With every wingbeat, a blast of air struck Jack and Ruby, and they had to struggle to stay on their feet.

One of General Gore's warriors, Jack thought with horror.

He raised the Shadow Sword. Ruby was bracing herself, ready to fight.

"I know that blade," the creature said. Her voice was so cold, Jack felt like someone had dropped ice cubes down his back. "It belongs to my master."

"It's mine now," said Jack, fighting back his fear. "And I'm going to use it to send you back to Noxx, where you belong!"

The creature bared her fangs. "I think not, Chosen One. I am Chiptra, and I have come to send *you* where you belong — to your death!"

With lightning speed, Chiptra landed on the ground beside the portal. Raising a powerful arm, she swung the chain and slammed the spiked ball hard into the ground.

The moment the ball struck the floor, a terrible wave of sound echoed from the weapon. If the noise of the terrawings' blasters had been bad, this was much worse. The sonic defenders couldn't stop it. Ruby sank to her knees, clutching her ears. Jack did the same. The sound was so loud that for a few moments he was completely deafened. All he could hear was his own desperate thoughts:

How will we ever defeat her?

CHAPTER 5

CHIPTRA'S BOMB

JACK TRIED to get to his feet,
but Chiptra swung the chain and
slammed the ball into the ground
again. Another wave of sound hit
Jack, knocking him off his feet. Ruby
lay on the ground, arms clamped
around her head. Jack felt like his
eardrums would explode. His head

was spinning.

The creature laughed. "Not so sure of yourself now, Chosen One?" she said in her chilling voice.

Jack watched a swarm of terrawings swoop down and circle around Chiptra. One was much larger than the others, with wings the colour of blood. Its eyes glittered cruelly. Jack guessed it was the terrawings' leader.

"We have done what you asked, Captain Chiptra," said the terrawing, its voice an ugly rasp.

"Good," she said. "So you've found the best place to plant the bomb?"

"Yes, Captain," the terrawing rasped.

Chiptra grinned delightedly, showing her fangs.

A bomb? thought Jack, horrified. *That must be the energy source keeping Hawk from contacting Team Hero!* His head had stopped spinning enough for him to move. He grabbed the Shadow Sword, which had fallen from his grasp, and crawled over to Ruby. Her orange eyes were wide with shock. Together they climbed shakily to their feet.

"Jack, we can't let them blow up the power station!" she hissed. "It's full of chemicals. The explosion would take out everything for miles."

It's not just me and Ruby who would die, Jack thought, his mind racing. *Hero Academy would be wiped out. Then there would be no one to stop General Gore ...*

The draught from Chiptra's beating wings made them both stumble.

"Stop these two getting in the way," she ordered the terrawings. "But keep them alive." She flew closer, until her face was right in front of Jack's. Her eyes were like empty pits, a black tongue flickering behind her fangs. "I want you and your friend to see the explosion, Chosen One," she told him.

"I want you to see the moment you lose and General Gore wins."

With a laugh of triumph, she lifted her vast wings and flew out through the doorway.

"He won't win, Chiptra! We'll make sure of it!" Jack yelled after her. He turned to Ruby. "Come on!"

They threw themselves through the snapping, swirling terrawings. Sonic missiles rained down on them, sparks shooting everywhere. Ruby was yelling something but it was lost in the noise of the fight. Jack swung the Shadow Sword, carving a path through the terrawings as best he could. He saw flashes of flame from Ruby's eyes. They fought hard, but there were so many terrawings that Jack and Ruby were barely getting anywhere. Jack panted, exhausted, calling on every ounce of strength from his scaly hands.

We'll never reach Chiptra, he thought in despair. *We can't stop the bomb ...*

Then suddenly the terrawings were flying away from him, screeching frantically.

"Did we scare them off?" Ruby asked doubtfully.

Jack looked around to see where the terrawings were going. They were diving into the portal, disappearing among the shadows.

"They're going back to Noxx," he said. He gasped as realisation dawned. "They're *escaping* ... Ruby, they must know the bomb is about to go off!"

Ruby spun around, scanning

Desolate Point. "But where is it?" she said desperately.

An idea came to Jack. "Hawk? Can you locate Chiptra for me?"

"Certainly."

The visor extended over Jack's eyes, a grid appearing over the power station. Data skimmed over it as Hawk scanned the surroundings.

"Fascinating," said Hawk. *"The chemical compounds here are really quite interesting, and highly explosive, of course—"*

"Never mind that!" interrupted Jack. "Find Chiptra — she must have the bomb! Hurry!"

Ruby asked her Oracle, Kestrel, to do the same. Data scrolled even faster across Jack's screen until a red dot appeared.

"Located," Hawk said proudly.

"Kestrel's found her," said Ruby at the same time.

They both raced towards the yellow reactor tower. Chiptra was perched at the top, tying the spiked ball to the scaffolding with its chain.

"Why's she doing that?" Ruby asked. She clutched Jack's arm. "Do you think …?"

He nodded grimly. "The spiked ball is the bomb."

Her work done, Chiptra soared down towards them.

"She's seen us!" Ruby said. She sent a blast of fire towards Chiptra, streaming from her eyes through the slits in her visor. But the creature swerved easily and hovered a few feet above them, her green hair coiling  like a nest of snakes, the blast from her wings making them stagger.

"Do not imagine that you can stop

the bomb," she said. Her icy voice made Jack shiver. "The chain that holds it was forged by General Gore himself. None can break it — not even you, Chosen One!" She gave a terrible laugh, her fangs gleaming. "Enjoy your last few minutes alive!"

With one more beat of her enormous wings, she flew over their heads and dived into the portal, disappearing into the swirling depths.

Jack started sprinting towards the reactor tower. No matter what Chiptra had said, they had to try to stop the bomb. Surely there was a way — and if they couldn't find it, General Gore would be free to conquer the surface of the earth, bringing darkness and terror ...

Ruby reached the tower first and began scrambling hand over hand up the scaffolding. Jack followed, heaving himself up with his super-strength. It was like the climb they'd made that morning up the cliff. Hero Academy and chasing robot spiders seemed like a lifetime ago.

He caught up with Ruby at the top of the tower of metal bars. Her face was set with grim determination.

The spiked ball didn't look like a bomb at all to Jack. It had no wires or buttons, just its metal spikes. But from within it came a sound that made Jack's stomach flutter with dread.

TICK. TICK. TICK.

It's a countdown, Jack realised. The chain that the bomb was dangling from was made of loops of metal thicker than Jack's arm. It was coiled and knotted around the top of the yellow reactor tower.

"How are we going to untie that?" said Ruby.

Jack was examining the bomb. "Hawk," he said, "can you see a way to defuse it?"

Hawk slid the visor out over Jack's eyes. Glowing data and calculations spun crazily across the display.

"I'm afraid not, Jack. The working parts are all hidden within the casing. Any attempt to open the device will set it off. It's rather clever."

Jack groaned. He tried to ignore the ticking of the bomb — it was getting louder, and his own heart was racing in time with it.

"OK," he said, "if we can't defuse it, we'll have to get it off this chain somehow. Maybe we can throw it in the sea."

"Out of the way, then," said Ruby.

Jack crawled away from the chain. Ruby's eyes flashed and, with a sizzle, she shot two beams of fire at the chain. Jack could feel the warmth of the flames and the chain glowed bright red where they struck — but it didn't break.

Ruby gave a cry of disappointment. She tried again, continuing the stream of fire for longer this time. The chain glowed white and Jack had to narrow his eyes against the burning heat. But it was no good.

Ruby slumped back. "Chiptra was right. The chain is unbreakable."

TICK. TICK. TICK.

How long did they have left? Surely it would explode any moment now.

Jack took out the Shadow Sword. He raised it above the bomb.

"It might just make the bomb explode," he said. "But I've got to do something."

Ruby nodded bravely. "Do it."

Jack drew back the sword. Then he swung.

CHAPTER 6

TRUST YOUR POWERS

TRUST YOUR powers ...

As Jack's blade arced down towards the chain, the words came to him. He stopped. Where had he heard them before?

It's what Ms Steel told us, he remembered. *On the cliff.*

"Jack?" said Ruby from behind him.

"What are you doing?"

Jack put the sword back in his belt. "There's another way to get rid of the bomb," he said. He held out his golden hands. "I think it's time we found out just how strong I am."

Ruby shook her head. "Look, Jack, I couldn't burn through the chain, could I? I know you're strong, but—"

"I'm not going to touch the chain — or the bomb," said Jack.

TICK. TICK. TICK.

"We need to get back down to the ground for my plan to work," said Jack. "And fast!"

The two of them scrambled back

down the tower. Jack leaped, his legs giving way as he hit the ground. Ruby landed next to him.

Jack pointed to the steel legs that held up the reactor tower. "Can you burn through those?" he asked his friend.

"Yes," she replied. "But—"

"Just do it!" Jack cried.

Beams of flame shot from Ruby's eyes, slicing through the metal. Jack ran to the bottom of the tower, gripping on to a bar of scaffolding. The flames died for a second as Ruby turned to look at Jack, eyebrows raised as she realised his plan.

Maybe I can't move the bomb — but I can lift the whole tower!

He hoped he could, anyway. The biggest thing he'd lifted so far was a car. Jack knew he was taking a huge risk ...

The tower shook as Ruby burned through another steel leg. Jack braced himself and took its weight. Ruby ran past him and began firing at the final steel leg.

Jack glanced up. The bomb was swaying on its chain — and now there was smoke coming from it. His stomach lurched.

This has to work. It's too late to try anything else ...

The final leg snapped. Jack's hands were now holding the entire weight of the tower. His muscles were screaming, his heart was pounding — but he'd managed to lift it.

Now he just had to carry it.

He tried to stagger forwards but his feet felt like they were welded to the ground. He squeezed his eyes shut.

Trust your powers, trust your powers ...

He could hear the bomb above him. *TICK. TICK. TICK.*

Grunting with the effort, Jack took a step forwards — then another, and another. He was carrying the tower!

TICK ... TICK ... TICK ... TICK

"Got ... to ... get it ... to the portal," he said, gasping.

Ruby nodded in understanding. She darted ahead, moving bits of old pipe and bricks from his path. "Go left," she told him. "Now straight on. You're nearly there, Jack!"

Jack staggered on. He knew it wasn't far to the portal, but it felt like the longest walk of his life. At last he reached the edge of the swirling black circle. Smoke was billowing from the bomb now and it was making a terrible screeching sound similar to the terrawings' sonic blasters. It was about to go off!

Jack summoned every remaining drop of his strength and hurled the reactor tower into the portal. He staggered as he watched it plunge into the swirling shadows, falling and falling, taking the bomb with it. A few moments later, he heard a distant *boom*. The bomb had exploded — but it had exploded in Noxx.

Just in time.

He collapsed in a heap at the edge

of the portal, exhausted. But Ruby sprinted over and pulled him to his feet.

"You've got to close it," she said urgently. "Quick, before Chiptra and the others can come back!"

Jack didn't need to be told twice. He drew the Shadow Sword. Somehow, despite his aching arms, he raised it above his head and drove the blade into the darkness of the portal. Black tendrils of shadow shot out, like the talons of a terrible beast lashing in anger. He and Ruby sprang back from them. They knew that being touched by the shadow would turn them into creatures of Noxx.

The shadows swirled like a whirlpool. Then, with a snap, the portal shut. All that was left was an ordinary stretch of ground.

Ruby punched the air with her fist and gave Jack her widest grin. Jack smiled back.

• • •

"My vision showed the terrawing assault on the school, but nothing about the bomb," Chancellor Rex sounded very troubled. "That explosion would have destroyed Hero Academy, Ventura City, and any chance we have of defeating General Gore. He has clearly become much more clever in his methods of attack. We wouldn't be sitting here now if it wasn't for you two."

They were in the Chancellor's study. After Jack had closed the portal, he and Ruby had made their way back to the jetty. One of the boats had gone — taken by Danny back to school — but they drove the other back to Hero Academy. Ruby had steered, giving Jack a chance to recover from lifting the reactor. Once they'd arrived back at the school they'd rushed to find the Chancellor. He'd been talking busily with Ms Steel but had called them in, saying he couldn't wait to hear what they had to tell him.

Ms Steel's face shone with pride. "We owe you both a great debt," she said.

Jack felt his cheeks grow hot. He couldn't believe Chancellor Rex and Ms Steel were thanking them, the newest students at the academy!

"Danny helped too," he said. "Is he OK?"

"Those sonic attacks really hurt him," Ms Steel said. "He was found collapsed by the jetty. But he's resting in the infirmary and he's getting better."

"Can we see him?" Ruby asked.

"I'm sure he'd like that," said

Chancellor Rex with a smile. "Then make sure you get some rest. I fear we have not seen the last of General Gore and his warriors, and we need all our best fighters to be prepared and ready."

Jack found himself grinning as he left the Chancellor's study. Jack Beacon, one of the school's best fighters? He'd never been the best at anything before. He couldn't believe how much his life had changed in just a couple of weeks.

Ruby's orange eyes were twinkling with pride. She gave his arm a friendly shove. "Come on, Chosen One. Let's go and tell Danny what he missed."

They made their way through the school. In the courtyard, Olly was leaning against the fossil of Raptrix, the Noxx warrior who had fought long ago.

"Back now it's safe, are you?" Olly scoffed.

"We're back now we've saved the school," Ruby retorted.

Olly gave a snort. "You two? Yeah, right."

Ruby gestured to the torn and filthy bodysuits she and Jack were wearing.

"How do you think we ended up like this?" she demanded. "While you were nice and safe here, we were being attacked by terrawings."

Olly shook his head. "I think you fell over while you were running away."

Jack slipped off his backpack, which he was still wearing. He shook it so it seemed to rustle. "I've still got a terrawing in here, Olly," he said. "Kept

it as a souvenir. Want to see?"

Olly quickly took a step back, his eyes wide with alarm.

Spluttering with laughter, Jack and Ruby crossed the courtyard.

"He deserved that," said Ruby. "I can't believe he thinks we made it all up."

"Oh, who cares about Olly?" Jack replied. "General Gore's the one we should be worrying about."

The route to the infirmary took them past the dormitories.

"Let's get changed before we go and see Danny," said Jack. "Meet you in five minutes?"

"Yeah." Ruby raised her fist and Jack bumped it with his own. She disappeared towards the East Wing dormitory.

Jack strolled to the North Wing dormitory, where he slept. He reached out towards the door handle — and saw something that made him stop dead. Words were written on the door in black paint.

GENERAL GORE IS COMING FOR YOU, CHOSEN ONE.

Jack's blood ran cold. *Who could have done this?* He looked up and down the corridor, but there was no sign of anyone.

Jack went through the door, looking to see if anyone was there. But everyone was out, training. Whoever had written the threat, Jack knew he had an enemy at the school – an enemy who was working for General Gore.

He clenched his fists, refusing to let fear chill his heart. He had his super-strength, the Shadow Sword and, best of all, his new friends. Whatever Gore had planned, he was ready to face it.

ONE WARRIOR WAS FROM THE DESERT
REALM OF SOLUS, ANOTHER FROM THE
UNDERWATER REALM OF SEQUANA, AND
... OTHER LANDS AROUND THE
M... ... HAD SPECIAL
... ... WELL

TIMETABLE

	MON	TUE	WED	THUR	FRI
08.00	ASSEMBLY	ASSEMBLY	ASSEMBLY	ASSEMBLY	ASSEMBLY
09.00	POWERS	POWERS	POWERS	POWERS	POWERS
10.00	COMBAT	STRATEGY	TECH	COMBAT	STRATEGY
11.00	MATHS	GEOGRAPHY	ENGLISH	HISTORY	ENGLISH
12.00	HISTORY	SCIENCE	MATHS	SCIENCE	GEOGRAPHY
13.00			LUNCH!		
14.00	TECH	COMBAT	COMBAT	STRATEGY	WEAPON TRAINING
15.00	GYM	GYM	WEAPON TRAINING	GYM	GYM
16.00	GYM	GYM	GYM	GYM	HOMEWORK
17.00	HOMEWORK	HOMEWORK	HOMEWORK	HOMEWORK	FREE

once a year at a secret tournament to practise their fighting
skills. Each of these warriors raised their own army of
soldiers to do battle against the Noxxians. But Gretchen
wasn't sure they were strong enough to win. Sh...
he greatest warrior of all ...

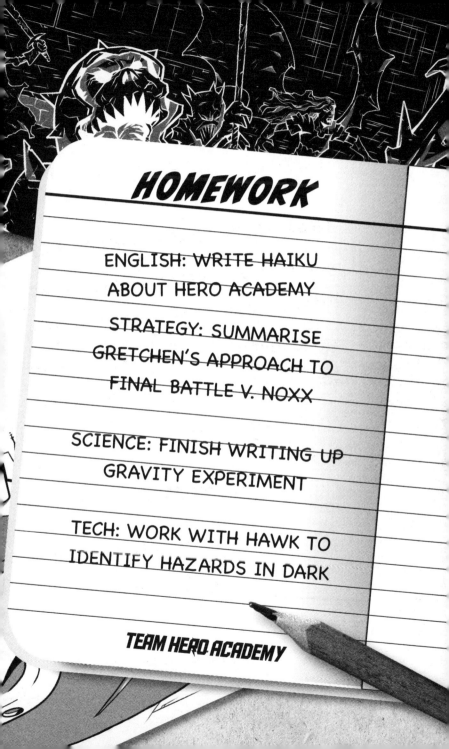

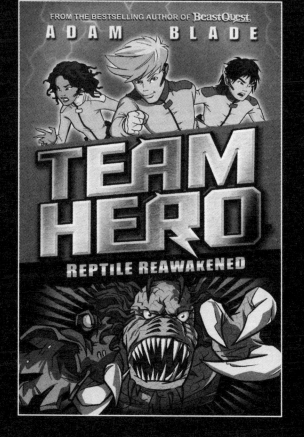

READ ON FOR A SNEAK
PEEK AT BOOK 3:

REPTILE REAWAKENED

CHAPTER 1

EVACUATION

We join the story as Jack and the other students are making their way to Hero Academy's courtyard, where Chancellor Rex will be making an announcement ...

Jack paused beside one of the school's towering fortress walls. Fossilised into the stone was the body of Raptrix, a lizard-like creature with a deformed human head and spike-covered back. Raptrix had been one of Gore's minions, frozen in rock since the last Noxxian invasion. Jack frowned.

"Guys," he said, "wasn't Raptrix's mouth closed before?"

Now the creature's long jaws were

slightly open, revealing needle-like teeth.

"You might be right," said Ruby. She stepped back suddenly. "Careful! There's broken glass on the ground."

Jack looked down at the glinting fragments, which were lying right beneath Raptrix. *Weird — how did they get here?*

"Maybe we should tell the Chancellor," said Ruby. "Hey, Danny — do you see this?"

Danny didn't respond. He was staring off into space.

"I thought his power was supposed to be super-hearing," muttered Ruby.

Danny blinked. "Pardon?" He shook his head in confusion, revealing large pointed ears.

Jack smiled, but it faded quickly. The sonic blasters used by the Noxxian warrior Chiptra and her flock of Noxxian terrawings had really messed with Danny's ears. The noise had been unbearable to Jack, but for Danny it must have been far worse. He'd spent the last three days recovering in the infirmary.

"Do you want me to get the school doctor?" Ruby asked.

"Er ... no — I'll be fine, thanks," said Danny.

Chancellor Rex was standing on a platform in the middle of the courtyard as all the students gathered, muttering to each other. Other teachers lined up behind him: Professor Rufus, the squat, red-haired technology teacher who could see through walls; old Mrs Hindmarch, who apparently had the power to summon tornadoes; and several others whom Jack didn't know. All looked grim-faced as the Chancellor began to speak.

CHECK OUT BOOK THREE: REPTILE REAWAKENED to find out what happens next!

WIN AN ADVENTURE PARTY AT GO APE TREE TOP JUNIOR*

WITH

How would you like to win an epic party at Go Ape! for you and five of your friends?

You'll get up to an hour of climbing, canopy exploring, trail blazing and obstacles and a certificate to take away too!

The Go Ape! leafy hangouts are the perfect place to get together for loads of fun and prove that you've got what it takes to be the ultimate hero.

For your chance to win, just go to

TEAMHEROBOOKS.CO.UK

and tell us the names of the evil creatures that feature in the four different Team Hero books.

Closing date 31st October 2017

PLEASE SEE the website above for full terms and conditions.
*SUITABLE FOR 4 - 12 years old, but open to any age child over 1m tall.

IN EVERY BOOK OF
TEAM HERO SERIES
ONE there is a special
Power Token. Collect
all four tokens to get
an exclusive Team Hero
Club pack. The pack
contains everything you and
your friends need to form your
very own Team Hero Club.

**MEMBERSHIP CARDS · MEMBERSHIP CERTIFICATE
· STICKERS · POWER GAME · BOOKMARKS**

Just fill in the form below, send it in with your four tokens
and we'll send you your Team Hero Club Pack.

SEND TO: Team Hero Club Pack Offer, Hachette Children's Books,
Marketing Department, Carmelite House, 50 Victoria Embankment,
London, EC4Y 0DZ.

CLOSING DATE: 31st December 2017

WWW.TEAMHEROBOOKS.CO.UK

*TEAM HERO Club packs
available while stocks last.
Terms and conditions apply.*

FIND THIS SPECIAL
BUMPER BOOK ON SHELVES
FROM OCTOBER 2017

Go Ape!
TREE TOP JUNIOR

BIRTHDAY PARTIES

at 18 locations UK wide

PARTY BAGS   🌲   **PARTY ROOMS**   🌲   **T-SHIRTS**

Find out more at goape.co.uk
or call 0845 094 8813†